Messy Bessey's
School Desk

By Patricia and
Fredrick McKissack

Illustrated by Dana Regan

SCHOLASTIC INC.

New York Toronto London Auckland Sydney
Mexico City New Delhi Hong Kong

To all the kids who made this title their first choice
—P. and F. M.

To Tommy and Joe
—D. R.

Linda Cornwell
Learning Resource Consultant
Indiana Department of Education

ISBN 0-516-23817-5

12 11 10 9 8 7 6 5 4 3 2 1   1 2 3 4 5 6/0

Printed in the U.S.A.

First Scholastic printing, March 2001

Messy, Messy Bessey,
your school desk is a mess.

There's wadded-up tissue
and paper clips,
colored markers
with dried-out tips,

VOTE FOR BESSEY

an old sack lunch,
a forgotten note,
scissors, tape, and
a poem you wrote.

**Your desk is so messy, Bessey.
See broken crayons, pencils, too,
library books that are overdue,**

rubber bands
and an apple core,
late homework
and so much more.

Messy Bessey had to agree.
Her desk was a disgrace.

So she threw away
the useless things, and
straightened out her space.

Bessey's desk was tidy now,
but something wasn't right.

16

17

There were other messy desks that were a terrible sight.

Come on, everybody.
Let's clean up your desks, too.

Bessey got the trash can
and showed them what to do.

23

Now all our desks are neat and clean.
Our papers and books are straight.

With everybody helping,
our classroom looks just great.

27

Cheers, Miss Bess!

Your leadership was excellent.

That is why we elected you
to be class president.

Word List (111 Words)

a	classroom	helping	now	showed	to
agree	clean	her	old	sight	too
all	clips	homework	on	so	trash
an	colored	is	other	something	up
and	come	just	our	space	useless
apple	core	late	out	straight	wadded
are	crayons	leadership	overdue	straightened	was
away	desk	let's	paper	tape	wasn't
bands	desks	library	papers	terrible	we
be	disgrace	looks	pencils	that	were
Bess	do	lunch	poem	the	what
Bessey	dried	markers	president	them	why
Bessey's	elected	mess	right	there	with
books	everybody	messy	rubber	there's	wrote
broken	excellent	Miss	sack	things	you
but	forgotten	more	school	threw	your
can	got	much	scissors	tidy	
cheers	great	neat	see	tips	
class	had	note	she	tissue	

About the Author

Patricia and Fredrick McKissack are freelance writers, editors, and owners of All-Writing Services, a family business located in Chesterfield, Missouri. They are award-winning authors whose titles have been honored with the Coretta Scott King Award, the Jane Addams Peace Award, and the Newbery Honor. Pat's book *Miranda and Brother Wind*, illustrated by Jerry Pinkney, was a 1989 Caldecott Honor Book.

The McKissacks have written other Rookie Readers® about Messy Bessey—*Messy Bessey, Messy Bessey and the Birthday Overnight, Messy Bessey's Closet, Messy Bessey's Garden,* and *Messy Bessey's Holidays.* They have three grown children and live in St. Louis County, Missouri.

About the Illustrator

Dana Regan was born and raised in northern Wisconsin. She migrated south to Washington University in St. Louis, and eventually to Kansas City, Missouri, where she now lives with her husband, Dan, and her sons, Joe and Tommy.

A COUNTRY MOUSE *and* A TOWN MOUSE

Retold by **Ruth Mattison** • Illustrated by **Max Stasuyk**

PIONEER VALLEY EDUCATIONAL PRESS, INC.

A town mouse went
to visit a country mouse.

Country
Mouse's
House

3

"Here is my house,"
said the country mouse.
"Come inside and have
some food to eat."

"Oh, yes! Thank you,"
said the town mouse.

5

"Here is some corn to eat,"
said the country mouse.

"Thank you,"
said the town mouse,
and he ate the corn.
"Please come and visit me
at my house!" he said.

The country mouse went to visit the town mouse.

"Here is my house," said the town mouse. "Come inside and have some food to eat."

9

"Here is some bread
and jam to eat,"
said the town mouse.
"And here is some cake
and honey."

"Oh, my," said the country mouse.
"Bread, jam, cake, and honey!
I like your food!
I like your house!
I like coming to town!"

11

A big cat came
into the kitchen.
The cat looked
at the town mouse
and the country mouse.
"Meow!" said the cat.
"Meow!"

"Look out!" said the town mouse.

"Oh, no!" said the country mouse.

The two mice ran and ran,
and the cat ran after them.

15

"Thank you for the food,"
said the country mouse.
"But I am going home
and *staying* home!"

TRADITIONAL TALES

SET 2

The Gingerbread Boy

Jack and the Bean Stalk

A Country Mouse and A Town Mouse

The Shoemaker and the Elves

The Ugly Duckling

The Teeny Tiny Woman

TRADITIONAL TALES

A COUNTRY MOUSE AND A TOWN MOUSE

Traditional Tales Set 2 ❧ Word Count: 196

PIONEER VALLEY **BOOKS**

pioneervalleybooks.com

ISBN 978-1-58453-552-2

9 781584 535522